Froodle

Antoinette Portis

A NEAL PORTER BOOK

ROARING BROOK PRESS

NEW YORK

For
Michael

Copyright © 2014 by Antoinette Portis
A Neal Porter Book
Published by Roaring Brook Press
Roaring Brook Press is a division of
Holtzbrinck Publishing Holdings Limited Partnership
175 Fifth Avenue, New York, New York 10010
mackids.com

Library of Congress Cataloging-in-Publication Data

Portis, Antoinette.
    Froodle / Antoinette Portis. — First edition.
        pages cm
    Summary: One day, amidst the usual chirps, tweets, and caws, a little
brown bird decides to try singing a new song and sets off an interesting
reaction.
    ISBN 978-1-59643-922-1 (hardback)
[1. Birdsongs—Fiction. 2. Birds—Fiction. 3. Individuality—Fiction.]
I. Title.
    PZ7.P8362Fro 2014
    [E]—dc23
                                                2013032417

Roaring Brook Press books may be purchased for business or promotional use. For
information on bulk purchases please contact Macmillan Corporate and Premium Sales
Department at (800) 221-7945 x5442 or by email at specialmarkets@macmillan.com.

First edition 2014
Book design by Antoinette Portis and Jennifer Browne
The art for this book was created with pencil, charcoal, and ink. Color was added digitally.
Printed in China by RR Donnelley Asia Printing Solutions Ltd.,
Dongguan City, Guangdong Province
3   4   5   6   7   8   9   10

Until one day, out of the blue,

Little Brown Bird
didn't want to sing
the same old song.

She didn't know what
she wanted to say.

But it definitely wasn't *peep.*

Something silly, maybe.

Froodle

sproodle!

Definitely.

Crow was not amused.

So trooo.
We dooo!

So Little Brown Bird said

Peep

But six minutes later,
something else slipped out.

Tiffle biffle,
just a little
miffle!

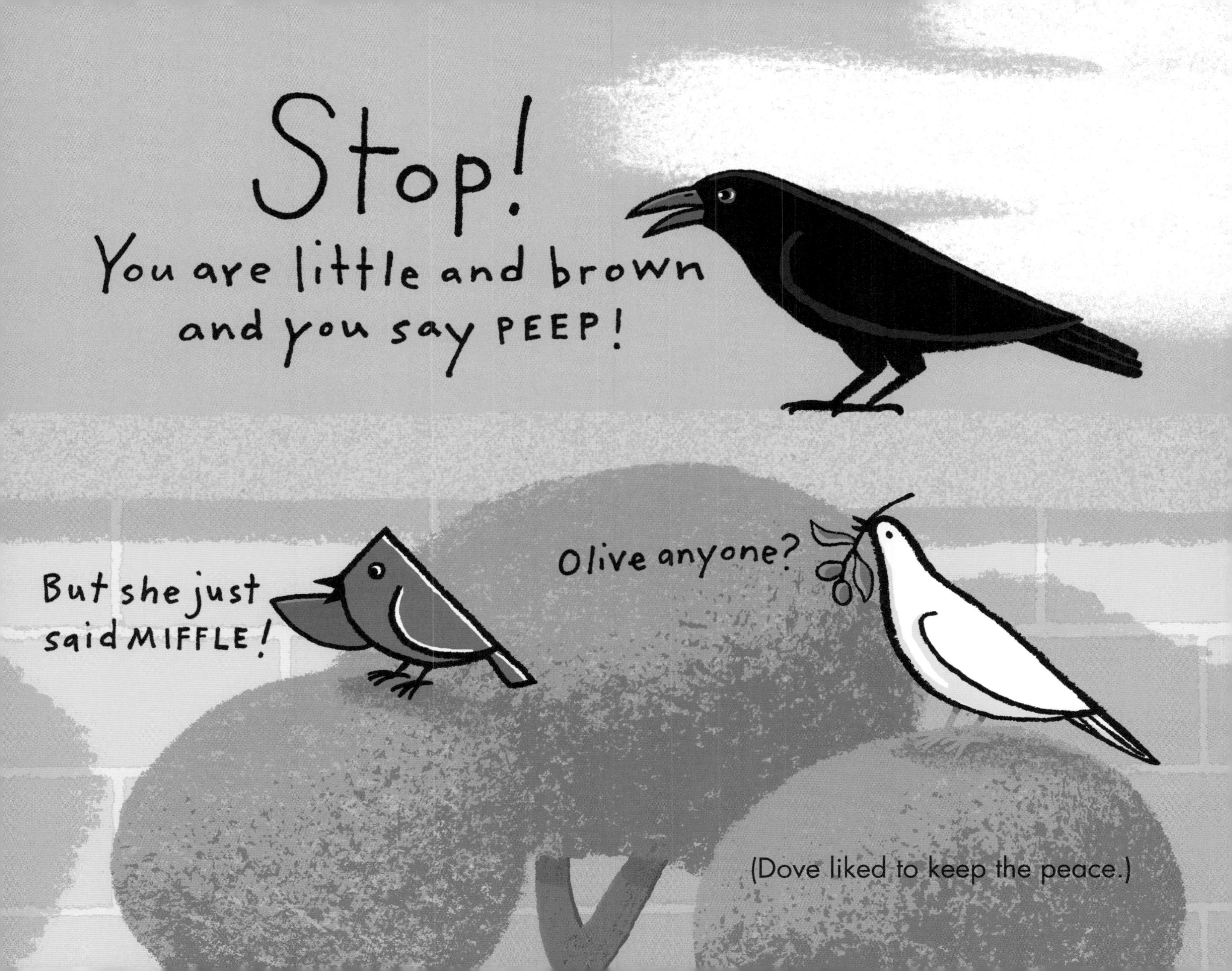

(Dove liked to keep the peace.)

But not even snack time stopped the silliness from spreading.

Because Cardinal figured out there could be silly red birds, too.

Ickle zickle!

Pickle trickle!

Now Dove was wondering
if there could be silly white birds.

Oobly snoobly!

There could.

Everyone knows there is no such thing

as a silly black crow!

Please come back!

But Little Brown Bird knew they wouldn't mind them forever.
So she wondered. Could crows be silly, too?

PPY!

Crows could.

The neighborhood was never the same.